Swirling Sea of Samsara

Poems from a Pandemic

by Nancy Winkler

Copyright © 2021

By Nancy Winkler

All rights reserved

Published in the United States

ISBN: 9798736877126

For Rama

Contents

At the Abyss	1
Blazing Buddha	3
Clorox and Compassion	4
Dukkha	5
Elevate	7
Fruit Fly	9
Gratitude to the Guardians who hold open the Gate	11
Hush	12
"I"	13
Joy	14
Kindness	15
Light	16
Midnight Moon	17
Now	19
OM	20
Perfect Peony (Pass the Purell)	21
Quest	23
Radiance	24
Sanctuary	26
Tantra	29
Unity	30
Vaccine	31

Wake	32
eXperience	34
Yes	35
Zoom	36
Epilog: Last Words	37

At the Abyss

Awash in an Atmosphere of Approaching Apocalypse

Adrift in an Aura of Alarm and Agitation

Anchor the Attention and Arrive Again

Acclimated to Aversion and Attachment

Afflicted by Anxiety

Afraid of Aging, Ailments and Ash

Access the Ancient Antidotes

Attune to Awakened Adepts Abiding in Awareness, Absorbed in the Absolute

Appreciate the Ajahns who've Analyzed the Aggregates and Advise us to Apprehend Anatta

Admire the Altruistic Arahants who've Abandoned Addiction to Arrogance and Applause

Alert to the Actual, take an Aerial view of Adversity

Be Amazed by the Architect and the Art:

>Apricots and Alligators

>Amethysts and Artichokes

>Asteroids and Acorns

>Apes and Angels

Blazing Buddha

Become a Bodhisattva for the Benefit of all Beings

Bravely take Birth in this Burning Bardo

to Bring Blessings and Brightness to the Broken and Bewildered

Be a Beacon of Brilliance

Breathe Buoyancy into Bleak spirits

Bathe us in the Bliss of Bhakti to Balance our Busy, Babbling Brains

Beguile us with the Bounty of Beauty:

> Butterflies and Begonias
>
> Beets and Bumblebees
>
> Bamboo and Bluebirds

Point us Beyond our Burdens and Blind Beliefs

to see that our Being is Bigger than the Border of our Body

Before we are Bleached Bones

Clorox and Compassion

Conditioned as Consumers to Cling to our Comforts

are we Capable of keeping Composure

in this Crazy Climate of Crash and Collapse?

Is it a Casual Cough, a Common Cold, or Catastrophic Covid?

Cautioned against Close Contact

a Cascade of Closures and Cancelled Classes

Cause us to Commune by Computer

We Can't know who's Carrying this Contagious Corona

Perhaps this is a Cosmic Call to Consider the Collective Community

to be Concerned about the Clinical Capacity to Care for all Creatures

to Contemplate the Courageous Caregivers working to Curb the Crisis

to Crack our Complacency and Cultivate a Clear Current of Compassion

Dukkha

Have I been Doomed by a Doorknob?

Am I Destined to Die from some Dreadful Droplet?

Or am I Doing enough Distancing to Delay my Departure?

Derailed and Discouraged by this Disruption in Daily Duties

Decide to Deal with this Disaster with Dignity

Without our usual Distractions

Diligently Discover how Delightful it is to Dwell in the Divine Dharma

to Deepen our Devotion

to Drop our Dumb Dramas

Diminish our Destructive Desires and

Dissolve our Dodgy Defenses

Diagnose the cause of our Discontent

Defeat our Disturbing Doubts and the Deceptions of our Daft Delusions

Time to Dive Deeply and Disappear into the Dynamism of life

To Dance with the Delirious Display:

> Daisies and Dandelions

> Diamonds and Daffodils

> Dolphins and Dragonflies

Disenchanted and Disappointed with the Darkness, find the Doorway out of Despair (but do Disinfect the knob)

Elevate

There's no Escaping this Extreme Epidemic

It's Everywhere

Elders are Existentially Endangered while those with Employment Ended and Earnings Eliminated are on the Economic Edge

Denial of Evidence, Excuses and Evasions, instead of Early Efforts to Eradicate, means we're not Equipped

Enough of Entitled Exhibitionists with Epic Egos and Eroded Ethics who Emit Evil

Establish Equanimity amid this Erupting Emergency

Be at Ease with the Ephemeral

Everything Ends Eventually Except our Everlasting Essence

Edge into the Experience of Eternity

Ease Effortlessly into Evolution

Evoke the Emissaries of Enlightenment who Embody the Ecstasy of Existence, who Encourage us to Extend and Emanate Empathy

Embrace their Enduring Elucidation of the Elements of Emancipation

Be Enchanted by what Emerges from Emptiness:

> Eggplants and Emeralds
>
> Eagles and Egrets
>
> Elephants and Earthworms

As footsteps Echo on Eerily Empty streets,

Expand

Elevate

Every moment has Enormous Energy

Be Empowered

Be Everything

Fruit Fly

On the altar

Fresh Flowers starting to Fade

yet still a sweet Fragrance Fills the air

White petals Float down and wake me from Forgetfulness

Form is so Fragile; all is Fleeting

What Force holds up the Feeble stalks that Fall ever so slowly Forward?

What Flood Fills empty space with Fantastic Far-fetched Forms?

    Frogs and Flamingos

    Fish and Falcons

    Freesia, Frangipani and Forget-me-not

Many things are best to Forget

Time Frittered away in the Forest of Fantasy

Foolishness; ways I think I've Failed

Funny how we Fasten to that which causes pain

Is Formlessness so Frightful?

Have Faith in Forgiveness

UnFreeze the Fixations

UnFetter and Flow

Filaments of sun Filter through the Frost on the window

The Fruit of remembrance is Finally Feeling Freedom

Fruit flies live just Forty days

Forty Flickering days to Fly

Gratitude to the Guardians who hold open the Gate

This Glittering Green Globe

Grows Gorgeous Gardens of Gardenias and Grapes, Goldenrods and Gladiolus

Grazing Grounds for Grasshoppers, Grizzlies, Goats and Gorillas

No Grinch, this Great Glory

Yet we Groan and Gripe

We Grow Gloomy and Grim

What Gives?

Glimpses of a Golden Glow

Go there

Shift Gears

UnGlue from the Grid

Give up the Grasping, the Greed and the Guilt

Glide into Gratitude and Glean the heart's Guidance

Gain entry to the Gateway of Grace

Hush

A Human is a Hologram Held Hostage by Habits

Too Hurried to Hear the Holiness of the Heart

It takes Heroic Humility to Halt the Hallucinations

Harboring Haunting Histories Hampers Happiness

Here are Helpful Hints for Harmony:

Heave the Heaviness

Harm no one

Hike in High Hills

Have Heaps of Humor

Hold to your Higher nature

Hope for all beings to be Happy

"I"

"I" stands for Ignorance

it thinks it's Important

it thinks it's an Island

but it's an Idiot

Imprisoned in an Illusion of Ideas

Invested in self Images

it feels Incomplete and fears its Impermanence

Time to Instigate an Insurrection

to Identify Instead with the Infinite

to Investigate the Intrinsic Illumination

be Immersed in the Innocence before Interpretation

Ignite the Intention to be Intimate with Ineffable Intelligence

Joy

Join with the Jailbirds

who Jumped free of the Jungle of Jousting and Jockeying

Jettison the Judgment and Jealousy, the Jumble of Junk

Journey with the Joyful, not the Jaded

Jam with Just and Jovial Jewels

(once they've been Jabbed by Johnson & Johnson)

Kindness

The Key to good Karma –

Kick up the Kundalini

Cut the Kite string

And Keep Kindling Kindness

Light

Locate the Light

Learn to Listen past the Labyrinth of Language

the Lowly Little Loops

Listen to the Light

Leap into Luminosity

Light a Lamp for the Lost and Lonely

(Like those Loyal to Lunatic Lying Leaders)

Life's Lessons can Lift us to a Loftier Lookout

if we Let go of the Luggage, Lose the Layers of Litter

Look through fresh Lenses at Life's Lovely Landscapes:

    Lakes and Loons

    Lavender and Lilacs

    Lions and Lambs

Laugh with Like-minded allies

Live in Limitless Love, the Link to Liberation

Midnight Moon

Maniacs are Making a Mess of things

the unending Madness of Me and Mine

Mired in the Mirage of self

Masters point to the Moon and remind us of the Great Matter

Mind the Moment

There May not be Many More Mortal Minutes

Meditate, Meet what arises without Mental Modifications, dedicate the Merit

Monks on Mountaintops with Mala beads and Mudras

immune from the Monsoons of Media and Marketing

are Merrily Muttering Mantras

and Moving beyond the Matrix of Maya

Marvel as you Meander through this Miracle of Manifestation:

    Monkeys and Meteors

    Mangoes and Manatees

    Minnows and Moose

Mingle with Music

Drink deep of the Medicine of Metta

Melt into the Mystery

Now

Did you Notice?

Every Now is New

    and Nameless by Nature

    before Needless Narrative makes us Narcoleptic

Every Now is Nourishing

    without Narcissistic Nattering and Negotiation

Any New Now

    could lead us Naked to Nirvana

OM

Ordinarily our heads are Orbs of Orbiting Opinions and Obsessions

Oblivious to our Original nature

But we can Opt to Overcome our Obstacles and Obstructions

by One-pointed Observation of an Object

or Openness

or living an Oath to care for Others as much as Ourselves

Obliterate Old and Obsolete Obscurations

It's OK to Own it when we're Off

Chant some Oms

Go Outside and be One with the Ocean

Find an Oasis, a higher Octave

Offer the world some Optimism

Perfect Peony (Pass the Purell)

I Perceived a Peculiarly Peaceful Peony

It's Pink-Petaled Perfection Permeated my Perturbations

and Pulled me to the Present

Paused in Praise of this Pleasing Plant,

I was Pollinated by Precious Particles of Perspective

Prioritize the Pure Heart

Purge the Predictable, the Patriarchal Poison

the Punishing Patterns that Perpetuate Pain

Be kind to People

Pelted by Plagues and Pandemics, this Place is Peppered with Peril and Panic

Pathogens Proliferating, Portfolios Plunging

what a Plethora of Problems

Passengers on the Planet, Perplexed and Petrified, need to Partake of the Positive, to Play in the Profusion:

Peacocks and Pansies

Pelicans and Prairies

Poppies and Pearls

There is Power in Practice; Profound Potential

So Pursue the Path Patiently

Pray for Protection

Pare down, Pack light

Prepare to be transPorted

Quest

Some Quests begin with Quirky Quotes

from the Quills of those who Questioned everything

who Quit the status Quo

with all its Quacking and Quarrelling

who Quietly Quelled the Quicksand of Quibbling and Quantifying

and cultivated the Qualities of their Quivering hearts

who made a Quantum leap out of the Quagmire

and into Quiescence

Radiance

For Realization to Ripen

Remember what's Really Relevant

why we Reincarnated into this Realm

Realign with Reality and Recognize the River of Radiance

Receptive to all that is Revealed

Feel the Relief of Releasing Restless Rumination

Renounce the Rehashing of Resentments

the Replay of Regrets

Retreat from Rehearsing and Reacting

Replace Rigid Routines

Relax the Resistance and find Refuge in Refined Rarified Rays

To Reawaken is Radical

Remain in Reverence to the Rebels Rooted in Rapture, Reflecting Reality

Rejoice in Rocks and Ravines, Rain and Raspberries, Roses and Reindeer

Sanctuary

So I'm Staying home, Sheltering in place, Slowing the Spread

The Sole Sentient being in my Space Station for Several days

Hence this Silly Spate of Scattered Syllables

Since it's Sort of Spring, I've Sprinkled a few Seeds in the Soil and hope to Survive to See them Sprout

We're in a Strange and Sad Situation, Stunned by Stark and Staggering Statistics, by the Scope and Speed of this Spread

Stuck with a Supremely Selfish and Spiteful Slanderer-in-Chief who's Surrounded by Slimy Sycophants who never learned to Share

Some Stressed Souls are Stampeding the Super Stores as if they're Starving, while Staffers Sanitize Shelves awaiting their fateful Screenings

Without a Sufficient Surge in Supplies to Save the Sick, so many will Succumb

Shortages of Sterile Surgical masks and Shields means we can't Support the Selfless who Strain to Sustain those Stricken with Symptoms

They Shouldn't have to Scramble for Stuff

Such a Shit Storm

Sequestered in my Sanctuary I use the Solitude to Search for Spiritual Sustenance

To Settle the self and Surf the Serenity

Sensitize to Subtle and Sublime energies

To Study the Sutras and find Solace in the Sacred Sayings of Saints and Swamis, Sages and Sadhus

I'm Surprised to Still be Standing and Somewhat Sane after Sixty-Seven years in Samsara

To Still see the Sky and not just the Sidewalk

I'm Sure it's due to the hours Steeped in my teacher's Samadhi

By Sincere efforts to Step into the Stream, Supported by Sangha

Staying inspired by the Sights and Sounds of this Shimmering Sphere:

    Seagulls and Seals

    Sunflowers and Stars

    Saltmarsh and Sand

    Sun and Shadow

Snow - especially the Sound of Snow

Tantra

Tense and Troubled by the Terrible Times?

Too Tethered to the Transient?

Try Training with a Translucent Tantric Teacher

who Transmits a Taste of the Timeless Totality

whose Touch can Transform Turbulence to Tranquility

who Tells you Tough Truths

on how you're Trapped by Tired Tendencies

and offers Tools and Techniques to Transmute them

Treasure the Teachings of Trusted True Tulkus

who Turn you Toward your inner Temple

Tune in to a Tribe of Transcendental Travelers

Take Tea and Talk Transparently

Turn the Tide Together

Unity

Unaware and Unwise

we Urgently need Unity

to Upgrade our Understanding

of the Universality of Us all

Focusing on Ugly Utterances

and stuff that's Unimportant

makes us Unhappy

So much to Unlearn and Uproot

Uneasy with Uncertainty?

Urge yourself to Unplug

Sit Upright Until you Unite with the Unconditioned

and let Unfabricated awareness Unfold

This practice of Unencumbering and Uplifting has so much Upside:

an Unshakeable Union with the Ultimate

Vaccine

Though covid hasn't Vanished

at least we have Viable Vaccines for this Virulent Virus

But there's no Vaccine for the Violence, the Vicious Vitriol

or the Villainous lack of Veracity

Nor for the Vanishing Variety of Vegetation

the Vacuum of Virtue

the Vacancy of Vision

As Voyagers here we need a Vehicle to help us Verify the truth of Buddha's 'Right View'

Vipassana, or Vajrayana or any Valued path will do

With Vigilance lower the Volume on the Vexing Voices of the Virtual world

Vanquish the need for Validation from the Villagers

Venerate the Valiant Visionaries who Ventured beyond the Veil

Value the Vastness, the Vividness, the Vibrancy that flows from the Void

Wake

We've Weathered another Winter

and Warmly Welcome back Wings and rushing Waters

Whistles heard through open Windows

Wishing Well for the Welfare of all We hear the Weeping of the bewildered

We Wince When We Witness the Whirlwind of Wrong and Wicked Ways

A few With Wads of Wealth While most are Without

The Worship of Worthless Widgets, Weapons and Walls

Wasting the Wilderness

When Will We Wise up to our one Woven Whole?

Walk a While Without a Wandering mind

being Wholly With each step

Without Wanting

We live in a World of Wonders:

    Wolves and Wildebeests

    Whales and Warblers

    Woods and Waves

Wordlessly Witness as Worries Wash Away

Withdraw from Worldly Winds that Wear us down

With Watchful awareness and a Warrior spirit Work to uproot the Weeds Within

Withering in Woundedness is not Warranted

Wisdom is the Way out of this Web of delusion

Wake to the Wonders that lie Within

eXperience

eXperts can't eXplain eXistence

It eXceeds rational eXamination

Only direct eXperience can eXtend our knowing

It's eXcellent to eXtinguish the eXtraneous

eXplore the ineXpressible

and eXalt in eXtreme eXpansion

and to not know what to eXpect

Yes

Yes, it's been quite a Year

Yet You didn't Yield to the Yearning for Yesterday

You ignored the Yapping and Yammering

and got on with Your Yoga

or Your Yardwork or Yarn

or built a Yurt

or cared for the Young

or learned how to Yodel

You balanced Your Yang with Your Yin

Zoom

Zoom makes me a Zombie

but Zazen in a virtual Zoo

is better than Zero Zen

Epilog: Last Words

The words began to vibrate and shimmer

To lift off the page and into the air like swarms of fireflies

Sparks of word shards dancing, tumbling

Letters changing shape

Unrecognizable

Some new alphabet being born

No more A through Z

I don't know this language

Nothing to do but sit back and watch the interplay of form and light

See what might drop into awareness from a place of not knowing

See what may be unshuttered in the lit dimensions of the hidden worlds

Made in the USA
Middletown, DE
05 September 2021